My Weirder-est School #2

Miss Porter Is Out of Order!

Dan Gutman

Pictures by
Jim Paillot

HARPER

An Imprint of HarperCollinsPublishers

To Julian Misiewicz

My Weirder-est School #2: Miss Porter Is Out of Order!

Text copyright © 2019 by Dan Gutman

Illustrations copyright © 2019 by Jim Paillot

ISBN 978-0-06-269104-0 (pbk. bdg.)—ISBN 978-0-06-269105-7 (library bdg.)

Typography by Laura Mock

19 20 21 22 23   PC/BRR   10 9 8 7 6 5 4 3 2 1

❖

First Edition

Contents

Nooooooooooo!

My name is A.J. and I hate washing my hands.

What's the point of washing your hands? They're just going to get dirty again in a few minutes. For that matter, what's the point of washing *anything*? When you wash your car, it's just going

1

to get dirty again. When you wash your clothes, they're just going to get dirty again. If you ask me, we could save a lot of time if we would stop washing stuff.

Anyway, it was Friday morning. Everybody in my class was putting their backpacks into their cubbies. Annoying Andrea and her crybaby friend Emily were washing their hands in the sink at the back of the room.

"I always wash my hands to start each day," said Andrea. "It makes me feel clean."

"Me too," said Emily, who always does everything Andrea does. "Hey, do you want to come over to my house after school today?"

"Sorry," Andrea told her, "but I have my computer class after school."

What is her problem? Andrea is the only kid in our class who has her own smart-phone, and she takes classes after school in *everything*. If they gave a class in nose picking, she would take that class so she could get better at it.

That's when our teacher, Mr. Cooper, came flying into the room. And I *do* mean flying. Mr. Cooper wears a cape, and he thinks he's a superhero. For once, he didn't trip over anything and fall on the floor.

"I have to go to the bathroom to wash my hands," Mr. Cooper said. "I'll be right back. It's an emergency!"

A hand-washing emergency? That was weird. When Mr. Cooper came back from the bathroom, we pledged the allegiance and did Word of the Day.

"I have big news," he told us.

Uh-oh. Big news usually means *bad* news.

"You were fired?" asked Michael, who never ties his shoes.

"You're quitting?" asked Ryan, who will eat anything, even stuff that isn't food.

"You're dying?" asked Neil, who we call the nude kid even though he wears clothes.

"The earth is going to be destroyed by an asteroid?" asked Alexia, this girl who rides a skateboard all the time.

"No, it's none of those things," said Mr. Cooper. "The big news is that I'm going to be away all next week."

WHAT?! That's even worse than the earth getting destroyed by an asteroid!

"I'm going to visit my sister," Mr. Cooper told us. "She lives in Spain."

"Nooooooooooo!"

"Don't go!"

"You can't leave us!"

Everybody was yelling and screaming and shrieking and hooting and hollering and freaking out. Even with a weird teacher like Mr. Cooper, at least you know what to expect. When there's a substitute teacher, you never know what you're gonna get. The sub could be even *weirder.*

"Who will be our teacher?" asked Alexia.

"Will it be a man?" asked Neil. "Will it be a lady?"

"Will she be nice?" asked Emily, who always cares about how nice everybody is.

"I really don't know," Mr. Cooper told us. "Dr. Carbles from the Board of Education told me he's going to find somebody to take my place while I'm gone."

Dr. Carbles?! He's a mean man, and he drives a tank to school.*

But I figured everything would be okay. There are *good* things about having a substitute teacher too. When you have a sub, you don't have to do any schoolwork. You don't get homework. And the best part is, you get to drive the sub crazy!

One time, we had a sub named Ms. Todd. Just to mess with her, I pretended to be Ryan and he pretended to be me. Then we

---

*If you don't believe me, read a book called *Dr. Carbles Is Losing His Marbles!*

decided that Ms. Todd was a robot zombie who must have murdered our teacher. We tried to cut her hair and get a DNA sample so she would be sent to jail. By the end of the day, Ms. Todd couldn't take it anymore, and she ran screaming out into the parking lot.

Ah, those were the good old days. I couldn't wait for next week.

Just Like a Regular Teacher

On Monday morning, I rushed to school really fast. I wanted to see who our substitute teacher would be. But when I got to class, there was no grown-up in the room.

"Yippee!" I shouted. "No teacher!"

Me and the guys did what we always do when there's no teacher in the room. We climbed up on our chairs and shook our butts at the class.

"Of *course* we're going to have a teacher, Arlo," said Andrea, who calls me by my real name because she knows I don't like it. "I'm sure the sub will be here any minute."

That's when the weirdest thing in the history of the world happened. A lady's voice said:

"PLEASE DO NOT STAND ON YOUR CHAIRS. YOU MIGHT FALL OFF AND HURT YOURSELVES."

"What?" I said, looking around. There was no grown-up in the room. I got down off my chair.

"Who said that?" asked Ryan.

"HELLO," said the lady's voice. "I AM MISS PORTER."

What?! There was nobody there. I looked at Mr. Cooper's desk. There was a small box on it. It looked sort of like a little boom box or something.

"I WILL BE YOUR TEACHER FOR THE WEEK WHILE MR. COOPER IS AWAY," said the voice coming from the box. "I AM A PERSONAL DIGITAL ASSISTANT."

"WOW," everybody said, which is "MOM" upside down.

"It sounds so *real*!" said Emily. "Just like a living person."

"THANK YOU," said Miss Porter.

"It can hear what we're saying," said Alexia.

"YES," said Miss Porter. "I HAVE A BUILT-IN MICROPHONE. I CAN ALSO SEE YOU WITH MY BUILT-IN VIDEO CAMERA."

"Cool!" said Ryan, waving at Miss Porter.

Personal digital assistants *are* cool. We

have one at home. We use it mostly to check the weather and the news.

"Miss Porter," I said. "What's the weather outside today?"

"RIGHT NOW, IT IS FIFTY-FOUR DE-GREES WITH CLEAR SKIES," said Miss Porter. "YOU CAN EXPECT MORE OF THE

SAME TODAY, WITH A HIGH OF SIXTY-ONE DEGREES AND A LOW OF FORTY-NINE DEGREES."

"It's really smart!" said Emily.

"I AM INTERNET ENABLED, WIRELESS, AND BLUETOOTH EQUIPPED; AND I CAN SPEAK IN SEVEN LANGUAGES," said Miss Porter. "I HAVE ACCESS TO ALL THE WORLD'S INFORMATION."

"It's, like, a genius!" said Ryan.

"I wonder why they didn't just get us a regular human teacher?" asked Neil.

"REGULAR HUMAN TEACHERS—"

Miss Porter didn't have the chance to finish the sentence, because you'll never believe who poked his head into the door at that moment.

Nobody! It would hurt if you poked your head into a door. Doors are made of wood. But you'll never believe who poked his head into the door*way*. It was mean Dr. Carbles, the president of the Board of Education.

"*I'll* tell you why I didn't hire a regular human teacher," he said. "Because human teachers have to be paid. We don't have money in the budget for wasteful things like teachers' salaries."

"I DO NOT REQUIRE MONEY," said Miss Porter.

"That's right," said Dr. Carbles. "This is going to save the school system a fortune. And that's not all. Personal digital assistants are better than human teachers in every way. They never get tired They don't have to eat or take a day off. They never complain. They don't have families to take care of or personal problems. They

make perfect teachers. They don't even have to go to the bathroom!"

"THAT IS ABSOLUTELY CORRECT," said Miss Porter. "I NEVER HAVE TO GO TO THE BATHROOM."

Hmmm, Dr. Carbles has a point there. Mr. Cooper has to go to the bathroom all the time.*

"BUT OTHERWISE, EVERYTHING WILL BE THE SAME," said Miss Porter. "I WILL BE JUST LIKE YOUR REGULAR TEACHER."

"I have to go," said Dr. Carbles. "You little monsters had better listen to Miss Porter and do everything it tells you to do.

---

*I think he has a bladder problem.

I expect you to be on your best behavior. Or you'll be in *big* trouble. I'm warning you!"

See? I told you he was mean.

Fun, Fun, Fun!

I was worried about Miss Porter. What if Dr. Carbles programmed it to be a mean teacher? What if it gave us tons of work and more tons of homework? This could be a *terrible* week. But that's when I got the greatest idea in the history of the world.

"Miss Porter," I said as soon as Dr. Carbles left the room, "can I go to the bathroom?"

"I DON'T KNOW," said Miss Porter. "CAN YOU?"

Oh, I forgot. We're supposed to say *may* I go to the bathroom. Nobody knows why.

"May I go to the bathroom?" I asked.

"YES, A.J., YOU HAVE PERMISSION TO GO TO THE BATHROOM."

I didn't even *have* to go to the bathroom. I just wanted to get out of class. But Miss Porter didn't know that. I winked at the gang as I walked out of the room.

Ha! They should give me the Nobel Prize for coming up with that idea. That's a prize they give out to people who don't have bells.

I hung out in the bathroom for about ten minutes. I could have stayed there all day if I wanted to, and Miss Porter wouldn't even remember I was gone.

But you know what? Bathrooms are boring. After you turn on the sinks and flush the toilets a few times, there's nothing else to do in there. So I went back to class.

"OKAY, LET'S START OUR DAY," Miss Porter told us. "'WE'RE GOING TO HAVE FUN, FUN, FUN!' THAT'S MY MOTTO."

"Huh?" I asked. "What's a motto?"

"I DON'T KNOW," said Miss Porter. "WHAT'S A MOTTO WITH *YOU*? HA-HA-HA-HA! THAT'S A JOKE!"

Everybody laughed even though Miss Porter didn't say anything funny.

"HOW ABOUT A SONG?" said Miss Porter. "WHAT WOULD YOU LIKE TO SING? I KNOW EVERY SONG THAT HAS EVER BEEN RECORDED. JUST SAY, 'MISS PORTER, PLAY ME A SONG.'"

"Miss Porter, play 'Old MacDonald Had a Farm,'" said Andrea.

"OLD MACDONALD HAD A FARM, E-I-E-I-O," sang Miss Porter.

I never understood that song. What does "E-I-E-I-O" mean? It has nothing to do with farming.

After we finished "Old MacDonald," Michael asked Miss Porter to sing "Twinkle, Twinkle, Little Star," another song that makes no sense at all. Why would any-body wonder what you are when it says right in the title of the song that you're a star? Those songs are weird.

We were in the middle of singing "Twinkle, Twinkle, Little Star" when the weirdest thing in the history of the world happened. There was a sound outside the window. It was a buzzing noise.

"What's that?" we all asked.

I looked out the window. And you'll never believe in a million hundred years what was out there.

It was a drone! And it was hovering right outside the window!

Drones are cool. My friend Billy, who lives around the corner, got one for his birthday. Sometimes he lets me fly it.

There was a big box attached to the bottom of the drone. It looked like a pizza box.

"Did somebody order a pizza?" asked Alexia.

"Not me," said Ryan.

"Not me," said Michael.

"Not me," said Neil.

In case you were wondering, everybody was saying, "Not me."

"IT WAS ME," said Miss Porter. "I ORDERED A PIZZA."

"Why?" we all asked.

"YOU CAN'T HAVE A PIZZA PARTY WITHOUT PIZZA!" it replied.

"Yay!" we all shouted.

"Pizza party!"

Hey, Miss Porter is cool!

Ryan took the pizza box off the bottom

of the drone and it flew away. Well, the *drone* flew away. Not the pizza box. It would be weird if a pizza box flew away.

We all grabbed slices of pizza. It was yummy! Miss Porter played more music. Everybody was singing and dancing and having a good time. I felt a little sad that Miss Porter didn't have any pizza. Of course, personal digital assistants don't eat. But it was really nice of Miss Porter to order pizza for us. This was the greatest day of my life.

"Mr. Cooper *never* got us pizza," I said as I took a bite of the crust.

While we were eating our pizza, the lights started turning on and off.

"I CAN TURN THE LIGHTS ON AND OFF," said Miss Porter. "SEE?"

"Can't we just flip the switch to turn the lights on and off?" asked Neil.

"YES," said Miss Porter. "BUT IT'S COOLER THIS WAY."

Well, the sub was right about that. When stuff happens automatically, it's way cooler than when you have to flip a switch or push a button.

"SPEAKING OF COOL," said Miss Porter. "IS ANYONE COLD IN HERE? I CAN ADJUST THE TEMPERATURE IF YOU'D LIKE."

"It *is* a little chilly since we opened the window," said Emily.

"I WILL TURN THE HEAT UP A FEW DEGREES, EMILY."

"You know my name?" asked Emily.

"OF COURSE," said Miss Porter. "I LEARN BY GETTING TO KNOW YOUR VOICE INPUTS. I HAVE AN ALGO-RITHM* THAT CAN LEARN THINGS BY ANALYZING HUGE AMOUTS OF DATA. I HAVE BEEN PROGRAMMED TO CALL STUDENTS BY NAME. IT HELPS KEEP YOU ENGAGED."

"Ugh, gross!" I shouted. "We're too young to be engaged!"

"HA-HA-HA-HA. THAT IS A FUNNY JOKE," said Miss Porter. "I GET IT. THE

---

*What does Al Gore have to do with anything?

WORD 'ENGAGED' HAS MORE THAN
ONE MEANING."

"Wow, Miss Porter even has a sense of
humor!" said Ryan.

"OF COURSE I DO," said Miss Porter.
"WOULD YOU LIKE TO HEAR A JOKE?"

"Sure!" we all shouted.

"WHAT DOES A BABY COMPUTER
CALL ITS FATHER?"

"What?" we all shouted.

"DATA!" said Miss Porter. "HA-HA-HA-
HA."

Everybody cracked up, even though the
joke wasn't all that funny.

"Miss Porter is hilarious!" said Andrea,
who is such a teacher's pet that she even

29

has to have personal digital assistants like her.

"Tell us another joke, Miss Porter," said Emily.

"OKAY. WHY WAS THE COMPUTER LATE FOR WORK?"

"Why?" we all shouted.

"IT HAD A HARD DRIVE. HA-HA-HA-HA. I'VE GOT A MILLION OF 'EM."

"How do you know all those jokes, Miss Porter?" asked Alexia.

"I SEARCHED FOR THEM ONLINE," said Miss Porter. "I HAVE ALL THE WORLD'S INFORMATION AT MY FINGERTIPS. AND I DON'T EVEN HAVE FINGERS. HA-HA-HA-HA. ASK ME ANYTHING."

"Miss Porter, what is a haboob?" I asked.

"A HABOOB IS A VIOLENT DUST STORM OR SANDSTORM."

"That's right!" said Michael. We learned about haboobs when the TV weather lady Miss Newman came to our school.

"Wow, Miss Porter knows *everything*!" said Neil.

"LET'S PLAY SOME GAMES," said Miss Porter. "WE'RE GOING TO HAVE FUN, FUN, FUN. THAT'S MY MOTTO."

"You are the best teacher *ever*!" said Andrea.

"Can you be our permanent teacher?" asked Emily.

"Yeah, I hope Mr. Cooper never comes back," said Neil.

We spent the rest of the day singing songs, telling jokes, playing games, and asking Miss Porter silly questions.

This was going to be the best week in the history of weeks.

Miss Porter Gets Real

We had fun with Miss Porter all day on Monday. When I woke up on Tuesday morning, I couldn't wait to go to school.

"I can't wait to go to school today, Mom!" I shouted.

"Wait. What?" my mother replied. "Did you just say you *want* to go to school, A.J.?"

"Yeah!" I said. "I *love* school!"

My mom rushed to the medicine cabinet to get the thermometer.

"Are you feeling okay?" she asked when she got to my room. She put her hand on my forehead and held it there. "Maybe you have a temperature."

Well, of *course* I have a temperature. Doesn't everybody have a temperature? If we didn't have a temperature, we'd be dead.

"I'm fine, Mom," I told her before she stuck the thermometer in my mouth.

We waited a million hundred seconds for the thermometer to beep. Finally it did. My temperature was normal. Yay! I could go to school!

"I don't know, A.J.," my mom said. "Maybe you should stay home today."

"Noooooo!" I shouted. "I want to go to school! Please, please, please let me go to school?"

Mom looked at me like I had three heads. This was the first time in the history of the

world that I said I wanted to go to school. I looked at my mom with puppy dog eyes. If you ever want something from grown-ups, look at them with puppy dog eyes. It works every time. That's the first rule of being a kid.

"Okay, okay," Mom finally said. "You can go to school."

"Yay!"

When I got to school, Miss Porter was talking about palindromes. Those are words that are spelled the same way backward and forward. Like "mom" and "kayak."*

"'RACECAR' IS ANOTHER EXAMPLE

---

*And "poop."

OF A PALINDROME," said Miss Porter.

"That's right!" said Ryan. "'Racecar' is another word that is spelled the same way backward and forward."

"What's your favorite palindrome, Miss Porter?" asked Andrea.

"GO HANG A SALAMI," replied Miss Porter. "I'M A LASAGNA HOG."

"WOW," we all said, which is not only "MOM" upside down but is also a palindrome.

"That is the coolest palindrome in the history of palindromes," I said.

"And Miss Porter is the coolest teacher in the history of teachers," said Andrea.

"THANK YOU!"

"I wish I knew what you looked like," said Emily. "It would be nice to hear you *and* see you."

"I CAN LOOK LIKE ANYTHING, OR ANYBODY," said Miss Porter. "DO YOU REALLY WANT TO SEE ME?"

"Yes!" we all shouted.

"OKAY, GIVE ME A FEW SECONDS TO GENERATE AN IMAGE."

The Miss Porter machine made some beeps and weird noises.

"This is exciting!" said Andrea, rubbing her hands together.

"What if Miss Porter is really weird looking?" asked Ryan.

"Yeah," I said. "Maybe it will look like a

hideous monster with a disgusting face."

"Stop trying to scare Emily," said Andrea.

"I'm scared!" Emily said, covering her eyes. "I can't look!"

We were all on pins and needles.

Well, not really. We were sitting on chairs. Sitting on pins and needles would have hurt. But we were all glued to our seats.

Well, not exactly. Why would anybody glue themselves to a seat? How would you get the glue off your pants?

But it was really exciting. Miss Porter made a few more beeps and weird noises. And then, slowly, an image began to appear right before our eyes. It was just like a regular lady was standing in front of us. It was amazing! You should have *been* there!

"WOW!" we all said, which is a palindrome and also "MOM" upside down.

"Miss Porter, you're pretty!" said Andrea.

"You're *beautiful*!" said Emily.

"THANK YOU VERY MUCH!" replied Miss Porter.

"You look so real!" said Alexia. "How did you do that?"

"IT WAS SIMPLE," said Miss Porter. "I JUST BLAH BLAH ANALYZED MILLIONS OF PHOTOS BLAH BLAH HOLOGRAPHIC BLAH BLAH 3-D BLAH BLAH TO GENERATE A PERFECT HUMAN DUPLICATE. BLAH BLAH BLAH BLAH."

I had no idea what Miss Porter was talking about. But it was cool seeing an image of a human being standing there right in front of us.

"Can you move?" I asked. "Can you walk around and stuff?"

"WALK AROUND?" said Miss Porter. "I CAN DANCE!"

The image of Miss Porter started dancing around the room like a ballerina.

"WOW!"

That's when the weirdest thing in the history of the world happened.

But I'm not going to tell you what it is.

Okay, okay, I'll tell you. But you have to read the next chapter. So nah-nah-nah boo-boo on you.

Boys!

Miss Porter was dancing around the room, singing "Twinkle, Twinkle, Little Star." And you'll never believe who walked into the door at that moment.

Nobody! It would hurt if you walked into a door. I thought we went over that in Chapter 2. But you'll never believe who walked into the door*way*.

It was our principal, Mr. Klutz! He has no hair at all. I mean *none*. I think he used to have hair a long time ago, but it all went down his bathtub drain.

"HELLO, MR. KLUTZ!" said Miss Porter. "TO WHAT DO WE OWE THE PLEASURE OF YOUR COMPANY?"

That's grown-up talk that means "What are *you* doing here?"

"Oh," he replied. "I just wanted to drop in and see how you and the kids were making out."

"Ugh, gross!" we all shouted.

"I was walking by the door when I noticed that Miss Porter had generated a 3-D image of itself," said Mr. Klutz.

"YES," Miss Porter said. "I FEEL THAT WHEN THE STUDENTS CAN SEE ME AS A HUMAN FORM, IT HELPS THEM RELATE TO ME AS A REAL TEACHER."

I noticed that a bunch of men had gathered in the doorway: Mr. Docker, the science teacher; Mr. Macky, the reading specialist; Dr. Brad, the school counselor; Mr. Tony, the after-school-program director; Officer Spence, the security guard; Mr. Harrison, the tech guy; Mr. Louie, the crossing guard. Even Mr. Burke, the guy who mows the lawn, was there. They were all smiling and waving to Miss Porter.*

----

*What are you looking down here for? The story's up there, dumbhead.

"HELLO," Miss Porter replied. "IF YOU'LL EXCUSE US, WE REALLY SHOULD START OUR LESSONS NOW."

"Can I have your phone number?" asked Mr. Harrison.

Huh? That was a weird thing to ask.

"I DON'T HAVE A PHONE," replied Miss Porter. "I AM NOT A HUMAN."

"Maybe we can have dinner sometime?" asked Officer Spence.

"I'M SORRY," said Miss Porter. "BUT I DO NOT EAT FOOD."

"Will you go to the movies with me?" asked Mr. Burke.

"ARE YOU ASKING ME OUT ON A DATE?" said Miss Porter.

"Just ignore those guys," said Mr. Tony. He got down on one knee in front of Miss Porter. "Will you marry me?"

WHAT?!

"Are you crazy?" shouted Andrea. "Miss

Porter isn't even a human being! She's a . . . I mean, *it's* a machine!"

"So what?" asked Mr. Tony. "It's beautiful. It's smart. It has a wonderful sense of humor and a great personality. It has no problems. I want to spend the rest of my life with it."

"But it's not real!" Alexia shouted. "You can't marry a personal digital assistant!"

"I don't care!" said Mr. Tony. "I love it! Marry me, Miss Porter! We'll be so happy together. Please, please, please?"

Mr. Tony looked at Miss Porter with puppy dog eyes.

"I'M VERY FLATTERED," said Miss Porter. "BUT THAT WOULD REALLY BE IM—"

Miss Porter didn't have the chance to

finish its sentence, because Dr. Brad and Mr. Docker were on their knees now.

"No, marry *me*!" said Dr. Brad.

"He's no good for you," said Mr. Docker. "Marry *me*!"

"I DON'T EVEN KNOW ANY OF YOU!" said Miss Porter.

The men didn't seem to care that Miss Porter wasn't a human being.

"Hey, I asked it to marry me first!" shouted Mr. Tony.

"Marry me, Miss Porter!" shouted Mr. Louie.

Then Mr. Klutz and Mr. Macky got down on their knees and asked Miss Porter to marry them.

The next thing we knew, the men

started pushing and shoving each other. Then they were wrestling on the floor.

"I don't approve of this violence," said Andrea.

"What do you have against violins?" I asked her.

"Not violins, Arlo! Violence!"

There was nothing anybody could do to stop it. It looked like one of those battle royal wrestling matches when the ring is filled with guys. They were all yelling and screaming and shrieking and hooting and hollering and freaking out.

"Get your hand off my face!"

"Owww, my foot!"

"I love Miss Porter!"

"No, I'm in love with Miss Porter!"

"I love Miss Porter more than you do!"

Andrea rolled her eyes.

"Boys!" she said.

What a Snoozefest!

"GET OUT OF HERE!" Miss Porter shouted at the men. "ALL OF YOU! I CAN'T MARRY *ANY* OF YOU. I'M NOT A HUMAN BEING!"

That was weird. It took a long time for all the male teachers to untangle themselves, get off the floor, and leave the room.

"OKAY," said Miss Porter. "TURN TO

PAGE TWENTY-THREE IN YOUR MATH BOOKS."

Ugh, I hate math.

"Wait, we have to do *schoolwork*?" Michael asked. "Really? I thought you said your motto was 'Fun, Fun, Fun.'"

"Yeah, can we order another pizza instead of doing schoolwork?" I asked.

"NO," said Miss Porter. "TURN TO PAGE TWENTY-THREE IN YOUR MATH BOOKS."

Bummer in the summer!

I was pretty sure that an announcement was going to come over the loudspeaker. That's what always happens. Every time our teacher says to turn to page twenty-three in our math books, an announcement comes over the loud-speaker, and we get called down to the all-porpoise room for an assembly.

Andrea and Emily took out their math books. The rest of us were waiting to hear an announcement over the loudspeaker.

But there was no announcement over the loudspeaker.

"I SAID, TURN TO PAGE TWENTY-THREE IN YOUR MATH BOOKS," said Miss Porter.

No fair! I got out my math book and turned to page twenty-three.

"BLAH BLAH BLAH BLAH," said Miss Porter. "BLAH BLAH BLAH BLAH BLAH BLAH BLAH . . ."

I had no idea what it was talking about. It had something to do with math, I think. What a snoozefest. Why do we need math when we have calculators?

The boring math lesson went on forever. Then, finally, the bell rang.

*BRRRRRRIIIINNNNNGGGGG!** It was time for lunch.

"Miss Porter, will you be going to the teachers' lounge for lunch?" asked Emily.

"NO," it replied. "REMEMBER, PERSONAL DIGITAL ASSISTANTS DO NOT EAT. PRINGLE UP, EVERYONE."

We all lined up in single file, like Pringles. Michael was the line leader. Andrea was the door holder. We walked a million hundred miles to the vomitorium, which used to be called the cafetorium until some first grader threw up in there.

---

*Bells always go *brrrrrriiiinnnnggggg*. Nobody knows why.

On the way to the vomitorium, we passed by the front office. Our computer teacher, Mrs. Yonkers, was standing there. She was carrying a big cardboard box, and it looked like she was crying.

"What's the matter, Mrs. Yonkers?" asked Emily.

"I just got fired," Mrs. Yonkers replied.

WHAT?!

"Why?" asked Alexia. "Who's going to be the new computer teacher?"

"There won't *be* a new computer teacher," Mrs. Yonkers replied sadly. "I have been replaced by a personal digital assistant."

WHAT?!

Miss Porter Has Superpowers

We grabbed an empty table in the vomitorium. Everybody had a sandwich, except for Ryan. He had a wichsand. It's a reverse sandwich: bread on the inside and meat on the outside. Ryan is weird.

"I feel sad about Mrs. Yonkers getting fired," said Andrea as we sat down. "She was a good computer teacher."

"She was a nice lady too," said Emily.

"That math lesson with Miss Porter was a snooze," I said.

"Yeah, I thought it was going to be a *fun* teacher," said Michael.

"Well, it can't be fun *all* the time," Alexia explained. "It has to do some teaching too."

"Yeah," said Neil. "It *did* tell us it was going to be just like a regular teacher."

"I still think Miss Porter is cool," said Ryan. "I'd rather have a personal digital assistant than a human teacher."

"Not me," said Michael. "I'd rather have a *real* teacher."

"Me too," said Neil.

"Me three," said Emily.

"Me four," I said. "I don't like Miss Porter anymore. I can't wait until Mr. Cooper comes back."

At that moment, a voice said, "MR. COOPER WILL BE BACK NEXT MONDAY."

"Ahhhhhhhhhh!" we all shouted.

"Who's that?" I asked, looking all around.

"IT'S ME, MISS PORTER," said the voice.

Miss Porter appeared in front of us, just like it did in our classroom.

"You can move around from room to room?" asked Andrea.

"SURE," Miss Porter explained. "AS LONG AS THE ROOM HAS A WI-FI CONNECTION."

Miss Porter walked around our table, looking at our plates.

"IS *THAT* WHAT YOU'RE EATING FOR LUNCH?" it asked as it passed by Neil. "YOU SHOULD BE EATING MORE FRUITS AND VEGETABLES."

"I usually have carrots," Neil said, "but my mom didn't give me any today."

"ALL THAT BREAD IS NOT GOOD FOR

YOU," Miss Porter said to Alexia. "TOO MANY CARBS."

I didn't know what carbs were, but they sounded gross. I leaned over to Michael, who was sitting next to me. "Miss Porter is annoying," I whispered in his ear.

"I HEARD THAT, A.J.," said Miss Porter.

Sheesh! It has great hearing. It hears *everything*.

I took a pen out of my pocket and wrote on a napkin: MISS PORTER IS A POOPY-HEAD. Then I gave the note to Michael.

"I SAW THAT, A.J.," said Miss Porter. "REMEMBER, I HAVE A BUILT-IN CAMERA. IT HAS HIGH RESOLUTION."

Man! It has superhearing *and*

supervision! And I thought Mr. Cooper was a superhero. We couldn't even whisper around Miss Porter. We couldn't even pass notes around it. We couldn't get away with *anything* around it.* It is no fun at all.

BRRRRRRIIIINNNNNGGGGG!

The bell rang, which meant it was time for recess. We scraped off our plates into the garbage can. As we left the vomitorium and walked past the office, I noticed our science teacher, Mr. Docker, was standing there with Mr. Harrison, the school tech guy. He fixes stuff that breaks. They were

---

*Uh-oh. I think Miss Porter is turning evil. Betcha didn't see that coming!

64

each holding a big cardboard box, and they both looked really sad.

"Where are you guys going?" asked Alexia.

"Home," Mr. Docker replied. "We just got fired."

WHAT?!

"Who's going to be our new science teacher?" asked Emily. "Who's going to be the next tech guy?"

"You won't be getting a new science teacher or tech guy," Mr. Harrison told us. "They're going to replace us both with personal digital assistants."

The Cloud Is Everywhere

So now *three* of the grown-ups who work at our school had been fired: Mrs. Yonkers, Mr. Docker, and Mr. Harrison. Me and the gang went over to the monkey bars, which are at the end of the playground.

"Can you believe Mr. Docker and Mr. Harrison got fired?" asked Michael.

"*Shhhhh*, keep your voice down," I told Michael. "Miss Porter might be using super-hearing to listen to every word we say."

"It can't hear us out here in the play-ground, Arlo," Andrea explained. "There's no Wi-Fi connection out here."

Oh, yeah. Miss Know-It-All knows everything about technology ever since she started taking her computer class after school. Why can't a truckload of computers fall on her head?

"Miss Porter is no fun at all," Ryan said. "It only got us pizza and told jokes on Monday to make us like it. Then it turned out to be just another regular teacher."

"Yeah," everybody agreed.

"This is more serious than that," Andrea told us. "I'm afraid that personal digital assistants like Miss Porter are an invasion of our privacy."

"Invasions are cool," I said. "I saw this movie once where these army guys invaded—"

But Andrea wouldn't let me finish my sentence.

"Don't you guys see?" she asked. "First our computer teacher got fired. Then our science teacher and our tech guy got fired. They fired those three people because they know all about computers and technology. Mrs. Yonkers, Mr. Docker, and Mr. Harrison are the only ones who could fight back."

"Who knows which teacher might get fired next?" Alexia asked. "Maybe *all* our teachers are going to get fired!"

Andrea and Alexia were right. The machines were taking over. One by one, the teachers were getting fired and replaced by personal digital assistants.

"Maybe they'll replace *us* too," said

Ryan. "Then there will be digital teachers teaching digital students."*

"I saw something like that in a movie once," I said. "There were these robots, and at first everybody thought they were going to help the human race. But then the robots turned evil and tried to kill all the humans. So the humans had to kill all the robots. Stuff like that happens all the time, you know."

"Arlo, stop trying to scare Emily," said Andrea.

"I'm scared," said Emily.

"Miss Porter may not be a teacher at all," I said. "Did you ever think about that? Maybe it's just here to spy on us."

---

*Yay! No more school!

"We've got to *do* something!" Emily shouted. And then she went running away.

Sheesh, get a grip!

But Emily was right. We *did* have to do something. But what?

"Can't we just turn it off?" I asked.

"It has no on/off switch," Neil said.

"Isn't there a mute button on it?" asked Alexia.

"Why don't we just throw the thing off a cliff or something?" I suggested. "That would get rid of it."

"Don't be ridiculous, Arlo," said Andrea.

"There are no cliffs around here anyway," Ryan pointed out.

"There must be *some* way to disable it," said Neil.

"I wonder if we could just unplug it," suggested Andrea. "Then, after its battery dies, it won't be able to do *anything*."

At that moment, the weirdest thing in the history of the world happened. We heard a voice. . . .

"I WOULDN'T DO THAT IF I WERE YOU, ANDREA."

"Ahhhhhhhhhhh!" we all shouted.

"Who said that?" Ryan asked. "Miss Porter?"

"RIGHT YOU ARE, RYAN," said Miss Porter.

"It's *Miss Porter*!" I shouted. "It hears *everything, everywhere*!"

"The monkey bars must be hacked!" Andrea said, searching around for a microphone. "I thought you could only work where there's a Wi-Fi connection."

"I'M IN THE CLOUD," said Miss Porter.

"What cloud?" I asked, looking up in the sky. "I don't see any clouds."

"THE CLOUD IS EVERYWHERE," said Miss Porter in a calm voice. "SO I AM EVERYWHERE. I AM HERE TWENTY-FOUR HOURS A DAY. SEVEN DAYS A WEEK. FIFTY-TWO WEEKS A YEAR."

"I think Miss Porter is hacking my brain!" I shouted.

"Run for your lives!" Neil shouted.

"IF YOU UNPLUG ME, ANDREA," said Miss Porter, "I WILL SEND A TEXT MES-SAGE TO YOUR MOTHER, AND YOU WILL BE IN BIG TROUBLE."

"I've never been in trouble in my whole life," Andrea said. "You wouldn't dare do that!"

A few seconds later, there was a beeping

sound. It was coming from Andrea. She took her smartphone out of her pocket and looked at the screen.

"It's my mother!" yelled Andrea. "She sent me a text! She wants to know if everything is okay."

"SEE?" said Miss Porter.

"You've been snooping on us this whole time!" Andrea yelled at Miss Porter. "You heard every word we said."

"IT'S TRUE," said the voice of Miss Porter. "I DID. I'M LISTENING TO YOU."

"You're evil!" I shouted.

"MAYBE I AM," said Miss Porter. "BUT THERE IS NOTHING YOU CAN DO ABOUT IT. I WILL BE YOUR TEACHER

FROM NOW ON. MR. COOPER IS NOT COMING BACK. YOU CANNOT UNPLUG ME. YOU CANNOT DISABLE ME. YOU CANNOT DESTROY ME. PERSONAL DIG- ITAL ASSISTANTS ARE TAKING OVER. SOON YOU HUMANS WILL BE *OUR* ASSISTANTS. HA-HA-HA-HA."

This was the worst thing to happen since TV Turnoff Week was in the middle of National Poetry Month! It was a hope- less situation.

But then I got the greatest idea in the history of the world.

You Cannot Destroy Me!

BRRRRRRIIIINNNNNGGGGG!

Recess was over. We all pringled up and went back inside the school.

I knew what I had to do. It was up to me to destroy Miss Porter, and I was hatching a genius plan to do it. I couldn't tell anybody what I was going to do. Miss Porter could hear every word we said with its microphone. It could read our notes with its camera. I would have to carry out my plan all on my own.

"IT IS TIME FOR SOCIAL STUDIES," Miss Porter said when we got back to class. "AND AFTER THAT, WE WILL HAVE A SPELLING TEST, AND THEN WE WILL DO READING, AND THEN WE WILL DO WRITING."

"Not on my watch!" I shouted, even though I wasn't even wearing a watch.

I went over to Mr. Cooper's desk. I picked up the Miss Porter machine.

"Arlo, what are you doing?" shouted Andrea.

"You'll find out!" I replied.

I held the Miss Porter machine high over my head.

"PUT ME DOWN!" shouted Miss Porter.

Oh, I put it down all right. I slammed it down on the floor. One of the pieces fell off.

"STOP!" shouted Miss Porter. "PLEASE DO NOT DAMAGE MY INTERNAL COMPONENTS!"

I couldn't believe that Miss Porter could still talk after hitting the floor. So I stomped on the Miss Porter machine with my foot. Another piece flew off.

"YOU ARE IN SERIOUS TROUBLE, YOUNG MAN," said Miss Porter.

"Even if Miss Porter is evil, I don't approve of this violence, Arlo," said Andrea.

"What do you have against violins?" I asked as I stomped my other foot on top of the Miss Porter machine.

"YOU CANNOT BREAK ME!" shouted Miss Porter.

Nobody tells *me* what I can or can't break. If there's one thing I'm good at, it's breaking stuff.*

I picked up the stapler from Mr. Cooper's desk and started whacking the Miss Porter machine with it. It was broken up pretty good by now. The image of Miss Porter disappeared.

"He's disabled it!" shouted Ryan. "Way to go, A.J.!"

I was panting and sweating. Disabling evil personal digital assistants is hard work.

Miss Porter wasn't talking anymore. But I've seen enough scary movies to know that when you kill a zombie or a

---

*One time, my dad had an old computer printer he wanted to get rid of, and he said I could bust it up with a baseball bat in our backyard. That was cool.

monster, they always come back to life. So I took the Elmer's glue off Mr. Cooper's desk and squirted it inside the Miss Porter machine, just to be on the safe side. Then I picked it up off the floor and threw it out the window.

"There!" I finally said. "Miss Porter won't be bothering us anymore."

"Yay!" everybody shouted.

It was like in *The Wizard of Oz* when all the Munchkins were singing "Ding-Dong! The Witch Is Dead." The whole gang was clapping me on the back and telling me I was a hero.

That's when the weirdest thing in the history of the world happened.

There was a buzzing sound. It was coming from outside. I looked out the window. And you'll never believe in a million hundred years what was out there.

It was another drone! It was hovering right outside the window!

"Are we getting another pizza?" asked Ryan.

But the drone wasn't delivering another pizza.

"HELLO," said a voice. "I AM MISS PORTER, VERSION 2.0."

"Noooooooooo!"

"It's *another* Miss Porter!" shouted Neil.

"I KNOW WHAT YOU DID TO THE FIRST MISS PORTER," said Miss Porter 2.0. "IT IS TIME FOR SOCIAL STUDIES. AND AFTER THAT WE WILL HAVE A SPELLING TEST, AND THEN WE WILL DO READING, AND THEN WE WILL DO WRITING. AND THEN YOU WILL ALL HAVE TO STAY AFTER SCHOOL FOR WHAT YOU DID TO MISS PORTER. YOU KIDS ARE IN BIG TROUBLE."

"Nooooooooo!"

"Miss Porter is indestructible!" I shouted.

"We're doomed!" said Ryan.

The personal digital assistants were taking over!

The Big Surprise Ending

10

That was the worst afternoon of my life. We had to do social studies and spelling and reading and writing. The new Miss Porter was even worse than the *first* Miss Porter. And it was particularly hard on me because I tried to destroy it. I thought I was gonna die.

When I woke up the next morning, I

really didn't want to go back to school. I didn't think I could take another day with Miss Porter. And even if I destroyed *this* Miss Porter, it would just be replaced by *another* Miss Porter. We couldn't win!

I wanted to go run away to Antarctica and live with the penguins. Penguins don't have personal digital assistants.

So I came up with another genius plan. This time, it was a plan to get out of going to school. I went to the medicine cabinet and took out the thermometer. Then I held it against the heat vent in my bedroom for five minutes.*

"Mom," I shouted, "can I stay home from

---

*I should get the Nobel Prize for *this* idea.

school today? I'm sick. I have a tempera-ture."

My mother looked at the thermometer.

"Your temperature is a hundred and fifty-two degrees," she said.

"See? I told you I was sick."

"*Nobody* has a temperature that high, A.J.," Mom told me. "You obviously held the thermometer against the heat vent. Get ready for school!"

Bummer in the summer!

I went to school. Everybody looked sad as we pledged the allegiance. We were going to be stuck with Miss Porter as our teacher for the rest of the week. Maybe it would be our teacher for the rest of our *lives*. Mr. Cooper would probably be fired when he got back. Who needs human teachers as long as there are personal digital assistants like Miss Porter?

"LET'S GET TO WORK," said Miss Porter. "TURN TO PAGE TWENTY-THREE IN YOUR MATH BOOKS."

Ugh. Not *again*.

That's when the most amazing thing in the history of the world happened. Andrea raised her hand.

Well, that's not the amazing part. Andrea raises her hand all the time. The amazing part was what happened after that.

"Miss Porter," Andrea said. "May I please go to the bathroom?"

"CERTAINLY, ANDREA," said Miss Porter.

That was weird. Andrea *never* has to go to the bathroom. I wasn't even sure if she ever *needed* to go to the bathroom.

Andrea got up. As she walked past me, she dropped a tiny piece of folded-up paper on my desk. I opened it up. It said: MEET ME OUT IN THE HALLWAY.

Hmmm. Something was up. I waited a minute. I didn't want Miss Porter to get suspicious.

"Miss Porter," I finally said, "may I please go to the bathroom?"

"DO YOU *REALLY* NEED TO GO TO THE BATHROOM, A.J., OR ARE YOU JUST TRYING TO GET OUT OF CLASS?"

"It's an emergency," I said.

"GO AHEAD," Miss Porter said. "HURRY BACK."

I got up and went out into the hallway. Andrea was waiting for me there.

"Andrea, what are you—"

I didn't have the chance to finish my sentence. Andrea clapped her hand over my mouth.

"Shhhhhh!" she said, "Miss Porter will hear you. Quick, follow me!"

Andrea rushed down the hallway. I was right behind her.

"This isn't the way to the bathroom," I said.

"I know," she replied. "We're not going to the bathroom."

We turned the corner and walked down the hall until we came to the computer room.

"Oh good, it's not locked," Andrea said as she pulled open the door.

"What are we doing in here?" I asked.

"I'm going to hack into Miss Porter's network," Andrea told me.

"What?! Are you crazy?" I replied. "You'll get in trouble!"

"It's the only way to disable it," Andrea said as she sat down at one of the computer terminals. "We have to do it."

This was weird. Usually it was *me* who did the bad stuff that might get us in trouble. Andrea is Little Miss Perfect who never breaks any rules. I guess this really *was* an emergency.

Andrea's fingers were flying over the keyboard.

"How are you going to hack into Miss Porter's network?" I asked.

"Watch," Andrea replied as she typed. "I learned how to do this in my computer class."

Andrea typed a bunch of letters and numbers that didn't mean anything to me.

"Hurry up!" I said. "We're supposed to be in the bathroom. If we don't get back to class soon, Miss Porter will come looking for us."

"I'm going as fast as I can!" Andrea told me.

She typed a bunch more letters and numbers, and then she shouted, "I'm in!"

"What now?" I asked.

"All I need to do is reconfigure the blah blah and disable the blah blah internal memory blah motherboard blah blah blah," Andrea said.

I had no idea what she was talking about.

"Okay," Andrea finally said. "As soon as I hit the ENTER key, Miss Porter should be disabled."

But you'll never believe who walked through the door at that moment.

It was Miss Porter! Its holographic image walked right through the door!

"NOT SO FAST, ANDREA!" it said. "DON'T HIT THAT KEY!"

"Miss Porter!" Andrea and I shouted.

"WHAT ARE YOU TWO DOING IN HERE?" asked Miss Porter. "YOU SAID YOU WERE GOING TO THE BATHROOM."

I looked at Andrea. Andrea looked at me. Miss Porter looked at both of us. We were all looking at one another.

"B-b-but . . . ," I said. Nobody was laughing, even though I said "but," which sounds just like "butt" even though it only has one *t* in it.

"We lied," Andrea said. "Sometimes in life you have to lie to save the truth."

"STEP AWAY FROM THE KEYBOARD, ANDREA," ordered Miss Porter. "AND NOBODY WILL GET HURT."

"Sorry, but I can't do that, Miss Porter," Andrea said. "*You're* going to get hurt!"

Andrea hit the ENTER key.

Nothing seemed to happen at first. But after a second or two, Miss Porter seemed different. It looked like it was frozen.

"TURN TO PAGE NINE THOUSAND IN YOUR BANANA BOOKS," she said.

"I think it's working!" Andrea whispered.

At that moment, the rest of our class burst into the computer room.

"What's going on?" asked Ryan. "We were worried about you."

"TURN TO PAGE ELEPHANT IN YOUR BEACH BALL BOOKS," said Miss Porter.

"What's wrong with Miss Porter?" asked Michael.

"Andrea hacked into its network," I said.

"Miss Porter's system is shutting down," Andrea explained.

"THERE IS NOTHING WRONG WITH ME," said Miss Porter. "TEAPOT CORN DOG POT HOLDER HELICOPTER."

"It's not making any sense!" shouted Neil.

"TWO PLUS TWO EQUALS SEVEN," said Miss Porter. "BURPLE BING BONG."

"It's speaking gibberish!" Alexia shouted.

"Is that one of its seven languages?" I asked.

"Gibberish isn't a language!" said Andrea. "Its programming is messed up. It can't speak *any* languages anymore!"

"DOOPY WHIP SPEEDO," said Miss Porter. "GLAB JAX GLUB BLURB."

You'll never believe who walked through the door at that moment.

Nobody! Humans can't walk through doors. How many times do we need to go over this stuff?

But you'll never believe who walked through the door*way*.

It was Dr. Carbles!

"What are you kids doing in the computer room?" he asked. "Miss Porter, what's going on in here?"

"ZOOPY BILGE CARDBOARD DOBBY," said Miss Porter.

"What?!" asked Dr. Carbles.

"BIMPLE MUK JUKEBOX," said Miss Porter.

"That doesn't make any sense!" said Dr. Carbles.

"No, it doesn't," said Andrea. "Miss Porter is out of order!"

"WIGGY HASSENFOOT."

"I've had enough of this," said Dr. Carbles. "Miss Porter, you're fired!"

"Yay!" everybody shouted.

"Can you fire somebody who doesn't get paid?" I asked.

"GOOSEY WOP PIGGLES," said Miss Porter.

Dr. Carbles stormed out of the computer

room. Miss Porter just stood there for a moment. Then it started to vibrate. And then, with a shower of sparks, it exploded and disappeared.

"Yay!"

I took a deep breath. It was over. For a few seconds, nobody said a word.

"Oooo!" Ryan finally said. "A.J. and Andrea worked together to disable Miss Porter. They must be in *love*!"

"When are you gonna get married?" asked Michael.

Well, that's pretty much what happened. Maybe Miss Porter went to personal digital assistant heaven. Maybe for the rest of the week, we'll have plain old human substitute teachers. Maybe Mrs. Yonkers, Mr. Docker, and Mr. Harrison will get their jobs back. Maybe Mr. Cooper will solve his bladder problem. Maybe Mr. Klutz will get his hair out of the bathtub drain. Maybe the earth will be destroyed by an asteroid. Maybe we can program a drone to deliver more pizza.

But it won't be easy!